DALAN
THE DUCK

D.R. Melanson

WestBow Press books may be ordered through booksellers or by contacting:

WestBow Press
A Division of Thomas Nelson & Zondervan
1663 Liberty Drive
Bloomington, IN 47403
www.westbowpress.com
844-714-3454

ISBN: 978-1-6642-7973-5 (sc)
ISBN: 978-1-6642-7974-2 (e)

Library of Congress Control Number: 2022918251

Print information available on the last page.

WestBow Press rev. date: 09/30/2022

WESTBOW
PRESS®
A DIVISION OF THOMAS NELSON
& ZONDERVAN

DALAN
THE DUCK

2

Dalan the duck was a happy young duckling.

He had many friends to play with, and he spent every day chasing them in the pond while his momma and poppa watched.

When he went too far away, Momma would call him back, and he would listen quickly and turn around. He was a good swimmer, but he was really excited that one day he would be able to fly up into the sky with the adults. He imagined what it would be like to be so high and to look down at his friends on the pond. He would race with others, and he knew he would be fast. Poppa said that he needed strong feathers on his wings and that someday he would have them; then he could join the other ducks in the sky.

One day, Dalan met a young goose named Gallo around his age. Gallo asked Dalan what it was like to be a duck. "Well, I race my friends on the pond, and I go very fast. Someday I will race them in the sky," he told Gallo.

10

Gallo began telling Dalan all about what it was like to be a goose. He told Dalan that he would grow much bigger than him and that he would not quack but honk loudly- much louder than a quack. "When I can fly, I will be so high you will not be able to see me. I'll be past the clouds maybe," Gallo said proudly.

12

"Wow!" said Dalan. "That sounds awesome. I want to be a goose too. Do you think I can be a goose like you?"

"Of course you can," answered Gallo. "My poppa said I can be anything I want to be; I just have to believe. So you can too."

Dalan headed home to tell his momma and poppa his new plan. He was thinking about flying very high, even higher than his duck friends. He would fly past the clouds and look down to the pond far below.

16

"Momma, Poppa, I have great news!" he said. He told them all about the conversation he had with Gallo and that he decided to be a goose instead of a duck. He was so excited.

Poppa looked at Momma for a moment and then said to Dalan, "Are you able to change the shape of your bill? Are you able to change your quack to a honk? Can you make your legs grow as long as the legs of a goose? Look at Momma and me. We are ducks. You are also a duck. You will always be a duck, and that is wonderful because that is who you are. It is good to be a duck when you are a duck. It is good to be a goose when you are a goose."

18

Dalan listened closely and realized Poppa was right. He realized there were too many things he could not change. At that moment, he realized Gallo was wrong. No matter how much he believed he was a goose, he would still be a duck. He would always be a duck.

20

"But one thing I know," said Dalan to himself. "I will be the fastest, best duck I can be. I am a duck."

CPSIA information can be obtained
at www.ICGtesting.com
Printed in the USA
BVHW010303201222
654588BV00001B/1

9 781664 279735